Sofia the Second

Adapted by Andrea Posner-Sanchez
from the script "Sofia the Second" by Erica Rothschild
Illustrated by Grace Lee

 A GOLDEN BOOK • NEW YORK

randomhouse.com/kids
ISBN 978-0-7364-3238-2 (trade) — 978-0-7364-3239-9 (ebook)
Printed in the United States of America
10 9 8 7 6 5 4 3

Early one morning in Enchancia, Princess Sofia is practicing her square dancing. She wants to be ready for the Highland Hootenanny that afternoon.

"All my friends from the village will be there. Plus Amber and James are coming, and my favorite band is going to play," Sofia tells her rabbit friend, Clover.

There's a knock at the door. Clover hides as Sofia's dad enters.
"The duke and his daughter will be here any minute,"
King Roland tells Sofia.

"I thought they were coming tomorrow!" Sofia cries.
"Today's the Hootenanny!"

"I know, sweetheart, but their plans changed," says the king.
"And you said you would show Joy around the castle when she came
Sofia is disappointed to miss the dance, but she
knows she has to keep her promise.

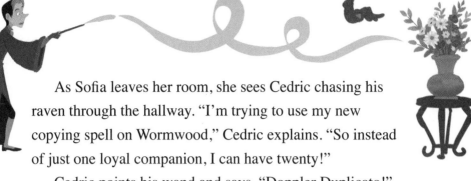

As Sofia leaves her room, she sees Cedric chasing his raven through the hallway. "I'm trying to use my new copying spell on Wormwood," Cedric explains. "So instead of just one loyal companion, I can have twenty!"

Cedric points his wand and says, "Doppler Duplicato!" He misses Wormwood—and zaps a plant instead. *Poof!* Now there are two plants!

This gives Sofia an idea.

Sofia rushes to Cedric's workshop and finds a spare wand. "I'll make a copy of myself so I can go to the dance while my copy plays with Joy," she tells Clover.

The bunny suggests that she practice the spell first. Sofia points the wand at an apple.

" Doppler Duplicato!"

Poof!

A pink apple magically appears next to the original red one.

"It's pink, but it looks just as delicious," Clover says.

Sofia points the wand at herself and says the spell again. *Poof!*
A second Sofia appears! She is identical in every way, except that
she is wearing a pink dress.

"I need you to play with a girl named Joy so I can go to the
village dance," Sofia tells Pink Sofia. "And please give her
this gift."

"I'd love to!" Pink Sofia says with a grin, taking the doll.

As soon as Sofia leaves, Clover takes a bite of the pink apple. "Yuck!" he exclaims. "This apple is rotten!"

"Just like me," admits Pink Sofia as she tosses the doll out the window.

Clover hops off to warn Sofia, but Pink Sofia grabs him. She locks him in Wormwood's cage and heads out to cause more trouble.

Pink Sofia spots Amber and James heading to the dance. She throws an apple in their path. James trips and falls.

"Sofia! Why'd you do that?" he demands.

"Because it was hilarious," answers Pink Sofia with a cackle.

Amber is surprised that Sofia would do something so nasty. She and her brother walk past her and enter the courtyard.

Meanwhile, the real Sofia is already there. "Hi! Ready to go to the dance?" she asks James and Amber.

"How did you get out here so fast?" asks Amber. "And weren't you wearing a pink dress?"

Sofia realizes her siblings must have seen her copy. "Oh, right. I changed," she mumbles as she rushes into the coach that will take them to the dance.

Sofia is thrilled to be at the Hootenanny!
She hugs her friends and happily dances to
the music. But then a new song starts.

The lyrics are about always keeping
promises. Sofia starts to feel guilty. . . .

Back at the castle, Pink Sofia is greeting Joy. "I am thrilled to meet you. Do you want to see my room?" she asks in her sweetest, fakest tone.

Along the way, Joy tells Pink Sofia that she loves her amulet. "Here, take it," Pink Sofia says, and she fastens the amulet around the little girl's neck. Cedric can't believe his eyes! He knows how powerful the Amulet of Avalor is and has always wanted it for himself.

"Now let's cause as much trouble as possible," Pink Sofia says. "We'll play tricks on people."

Just then, Cedric runs up. "Princess Sofia, how could you give your precious amulet to this little girl?" he asks.

Pink Sofia grins. "If you close your eyes and wish for it, maybe I'll give it to you."

Cedric does exactly that. But Pink Sofia pulls Joy out of the room and leaves Cedric there with his eyes closed.

"That trick was mean," Joy tells Pink Sofia.
"I just want a tour of the castle."

"Okay," Pink Sofia agrees. "But first, let's play hide-and-seek."

Joy skips down the hall to hide. Pink Sofia races out of the castle and into a coach. Pretending to be the real Sofia, she demands that the coachman take her to the dance.

Sofia is happily swinging from one dance partner to the next until . . . she is face to face with Pink Sofia!

"Wait—if you're here, who's playing with Joy?" Sofia asks. "It's not nice to leave her alone."

"*I'm* not nice," says Pink Sofia.

"You can call me

Sofia
the
Worst!"

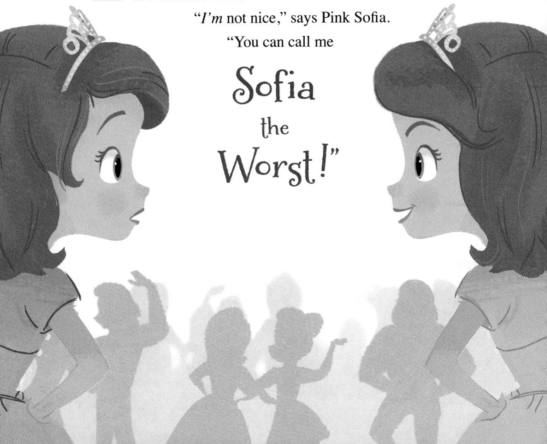

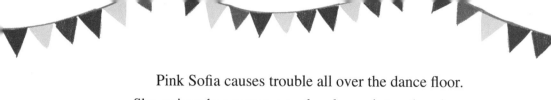

Pink Sofia causes trouble all over the dance floor.
She swings her partners so they bump into other dancers.

She stomps on people's toes.

She knocks off people's hats.

The real Sofia runs after her,
apologizing to everyone as she goes.

Finally, Sofia catches up to Pink Sofia and pulls her into an empty barn. "I have to go to the castle before my dad finds out that no one's playing with Joy," says Sofia. "And you have to stay out of trouble until I get back!"

Sofia locks the barn door and rushes to her coach.

Meanwhile, a castle servant spots Joy under a throne.

"I'm just playing hide-and-seek," Joy explains. "Princess Sofia is going to find me."

The servant looks confused. "Princess Sofia flew off in a coach moments ago," he says.

Joy is upset—and angry.

Nearby, Cedric goes into his workshop to think
of another way to get the amulet.

"Finally!" calls Clover from Wormwood's cage.
"Let me outta here!"

Cedric is pleased to see Clover. He takes the
bunny and offers him to Joy in exchange
for the amulet. She happily agrees.

Just then, Sofia arrives at the castle.
She thanks Cedric for looking after Joy
and Clover.

Cedric looks puzzled when he sees
the amulet on Sofia's neck. "Wait . . .
why are there two amulets?" he asks.

Before Sofia can answer, she spots Pink Sofia, who has escaped from the barn. She runs after her mean copy, and they both crash into her father and the duke.

"Sofia!" King Roland exclaims. Then he notices the other Sofia. "Sofia?"

"Yes, there are two of us," Sofia admits.

"I used Cedric's copying spell to make a copy of myself," Sofia says to her father. "But I wound up making a mess of everything."

She asks Cedric to reverse the spell. "Dopple-de-mimicus!" *Poof!* Pink Sofia disappears—along with the amulet that Cedric had finally gotten his hands on.

Sofia apologizes to her father—and to Joy. "We can do anything you want," she tells her new friend. Soon they are happily dancing at the Hootenanny!

"Sofia, I'm so glad I got to spend time with the real you," Joy says. Then a moment later she adds, "It *is* the real you, right?"

Sofia nods. "Yes, it's the real me. No more copies!"